Chinese New Year's
Dragon

by Rachel Sing

Illustrated by
Shao Wei Liu

ALADDIN PAPERBACKS

Aladdin Paperbacks, An imprint of Simon & Schuster Children's Publishing Division, 1230 Avenue of the Americas, New York, NY 10020. Copyright © 1992 by The Children's Museum, Boston. First Aladdin Paperbacks edition 1994. Originally published by Modern Curriculum Press as part of the Multicultural Celebrations Series created under the auspices of The Children's Museum, Boston. Leslie Swartz, Director of Teacher Services, organized and directed this project with funding from The Hitachi Foundation. All rights reserved including the right of reproduction in whole or in part in any form. Designed by Gary Fujiwara. Photographs: 2, 6, 14, Leslie Swartz; 20, Hong Kong Tourist Association. Manufactured in China

20 19 18 17 16 15 14
ISBN: 0-671-88602-9

Something special always happens for Chinese
people at the Lunar New Year. One year on the
dark night of the new moon, something positively
magical happened to me.

That year started just like any other year. When
Nainai began to scrub every corner of the house, I
knew that soon it would be the New Year. Nainai
says she cleans everything so that no bad luck from
the old year will follow us into the new.

Just like any other year, we got special calendars in
the mail from friends and relatives in faraway
places—calendars from China and Hong Kong and
Singapore and Taiwan. If you looked closely at
them, you could see the lunar date for each day
written in Chinese.

Just like any other year, we went to the markets where we buy special Chinese foods and decorations.

Just like any other year, there were *fu* signs everywhere. *Fu* is the Chinese word for good fortune or wealth. People hang the *fu* upside down for extra good luck.

Just like any other New Year, there were lots of dragons around. But this year there were more dragons than usual. This year there were dragons everywhere. This year, the New Year was going to be a Year of the Dragon.

I brought a dragon home.

Just like any other year, Uncle Min wrote *chunlian* with a brush and ink. *Chunlian,* which have decorated Chinese people's homes for hundreds of years, are always done in pairs. This year Uncle Min wrote, "The dragon waits for spring to come" on one strip of paper, and "Dragons make thunder and rain for fun" on the other.

Uncle Min read the *chunlian* to me. I'm just learning Chinese.

Just like any other year, Mom put out flowers. This year she chose narcissus. Some years she arranged plum blossoms in a vase. At New Year, people start looking forward to spring and new beginnings.

Just like any other year, I helped Nainai put out the special roasted seeds and dried fruits we had bought. Each one has a special meaning. Melon and lotus seeds stand for having lots of children in the family.

Just like any other year, the adults cooked all day
and all night the day before New Year's Eve. Uncle
Min roasted a duck and cooked my favorite pork
dish. Aunt Wang steamed a whole fish. The word
for fish sounds like the word for plenty in Chinese,
and we really had plenty for the New Year.

Nainai made little pillows of dough filled with
vegetables and meat, called *jiaozi*. The *jiaozi* are
usually made in northern China at New Year. To
make *jiaozi*, you press the sides of the dough
together. They remind people about friendship and
family togetherness.

And just like any other year, we had noodles at our New Year's meal—long noodles! Long noodles stand for long life. You must not cut the noodles while you are eating them. If you do, you will cut short your luck, or cut off a friendship, or shorten your life.

Just like any other year, New Year's Eve finally came. The adults played cards after dinner. My cousins and I watched them and played games of our own. Everyone stayed up past midnight to welcome the New Year.

13

Just like any other New Year's Eve, the adults gave us children red and gold envelopes with money inside, called *hongbao*. *Hongbao* means "red envelope" in Chinese. The money is called "lucky money."

But that one New Year's Eve, just as I was feeling sleepy, Nainai nudged my shoulder. She led me to my room. I brought my dragon kite with me. As I lay in bed, Nainai explained to me about the dragon and the Lunar New Year.

14

Nainai said that long ago in China, people believed that the dragon had power over all water. They believed that there were river dragons and rain dragons. The rain dragon made thunder and lightning when it crossed the sky.

Nainai told me that people once thought that the dragon went to sleep in winter and woke up in the spring, just in time to bring the spring rains. At New Year, people set off firecrackers to make sure the dragon did not sleep too long.

As Nainai talked, I suddenly felt like I was riding through the clouds high above the earth on my dragon. I traveled far away, back in time. I looked below me and could see a Lunar New Year's Eve in China long ago.

The next thing I knew, I was back with Nainai.
I could hear the laughter of my family inside.
Fireworks were beginning to go off. It was
midnight. The Year of the Dragon had arrived.

Glossary

chunlian (CHWUHN-lee-en) a pair of New Year's greetings written in Chinese on red strips of paper, that are hung vertically

fu (FOO) wealth and good luck

hongbao (HOHNG-bow) a red envelope containing money that is a traditional New Year's gift for children

jiaozi (j'YOW-dzeh) dumplings filled with meat and vegetables

lunar (LOO-nur) of or like the moon

Nainai (NEYE-neye) one of many affectionate nicknames for grandmother

About the Author

Rachel Sing grew up in a bi-racial family in the United States. She lived and worked in China from 1982 to 1985. She has taught Chinese language in an elementary school in Hawaii and at Wellesley College. A student again, Ms. Sing is now studying child development and curriculum design at the Harvard Graduate School of Education.

About the Illustrator

Artist **Shao Wei Liu** was born in Hangzhou, China, and came to the United States in 1982. Her art has appeared in newspapers, magazines, and on greeting cards. Ms. Liu currently works as a free-lance illustrator and designer.